Sweet
Memories
Still

Sweet
Memories
Still

To Peggy,

Natalie Kinsey-Warnock **1999**

Natalie Kinsey-Warnock

Illustrated by
Laurie Harden

Cobblehill Books/Dutton
New York

Library of Congress Cataloging-in-Publication Data

Kinsey-Warnock, Natalie.
Sweet memories still / Natalie Kinsey-Warnock :
illustrated by Laurie Harden.

p.   cm.

Summary: Although she initially resents having to spend time
with her ailing grandmother, Shelby gradually recognizes
that she has much to learn from this older lady.
ISBN 0-525-65230-2
[1. Grandmothers—Fiction.   2. Self-confidence—Fiction.]
I. Harden, Laurie, ill.   II. Title.
PZ7.K6293Sw   1997   [Fic]—dc20   96-7750   CIP   AC

Published in the United States by Cobblehill Books,
an affiliate of Dutton Children's Books,
a division of Penguin Books USA Inc.,
375 Hudson Street, New York, New York 10014
Designed by Charlotte Staub
Printed in the United States of America   First Edition
10 9 8 7 6 5 4 3 2 1

Books by Natalie Kinsey-Warnock

for
Jim and
Alene

Shelby looked up from her book as Dad came in from the barn, bringing with him the smells of cows, hay, and manure. He set a pitcher of milk on the table and grinned tiredly as Shelby's mother pointed to his boots and waggled a spatula at him.

"Run get me the bootjack, Shelby," he said. "You know your mother doesn't like me tracking up her clean floor."

As Shelby ran to get the heavy jack, she heard Dad and Mama discussing the day's events. With both of them working such long hours, Dad farming and Mama teaching second grade twenty miles away in Greensboro, some days the first time they got to talk with each other was while supper was being prepared. But now summer was here, and Mama would be home. It made for less money coming in during the summer months, but Dad needed both Mama and Shelby to help with the haying.

"That Jersey heifer freshened this morning," Dad said. Shelby had seen the calf, the color of a fawn but without the spots, and large nut-brown eyes.

As Dad pulled off his boots, a paper slipped from his pocket to the floor. Shelby picked it up and unfolded it.

Bold, black letters practically leaped off the page.

ART CONTEST! $750 IN PRIZES!

The Cabot Creamery is celebrating its 75th anniversary. The winning art work will be used in Cabot advertising. Entries should reflect the 75-year history of the creamery's existence and must be received no later than August 1, 1994.

"Where'd you get this, Dad?" Shelby asked.

Dad stripped off his socks and piled them on his boots. Shelby wrinkled her nose. She was used to all the earthy smells of the barn, but the stink of Dad's socks could kill a buzzard.

"Oh, your Uncle Earl just stopped by as I was finishing up milking and left one of those fliers. Seems as the creamery's going to have a big celebration and banquet. The television station is even going to be there."

Uncle Earl worked at the creamery. His job was to cut up the cheese curd so that the whey would drain off. Shelby had gone with him many times to see how he cut and stirred the curd in the long, gleaming stainless-steel vats, and how the curds were pressed into large blocks of cheese, then cut and waxed to age for up to a year. The creamery was famous for its cheddar cheese.

Dad filled his plate with mashed potato and pork chops, but passed the bowl of green beans along to Shelby without taking any. Dad was worse than any four year old when it came to eating vegetables.

"Why? Are you interested in entering?" he asked.

"Oh, Frank, don't tease her," Mama said as she spooned a few beans onto his plate. "I'm sure it's for adult artists only. Besides, employees' families can never enter contests like that."

Dad pointed to the paper Shelby still held.

"Doesn't give any age on there, does it?" he said. "And you and I aren't employed there. Besides, they're having the judges be from Johnson College, not the creamery, so I guess anybody can enter the contest if they want. Maybe Shelby ought to give it a try. She likes drawing, and she's good at it."

Shelby ducked her head, embarrassed but pleased, too. She knew she was good at drawing, everyone at school told her so: Mrs. Graham, Mr. Kendall, and even Mrs. Whitman, the principal. They were always trying to get her to design posters, or the covers for the school budget reports, or scenery for plays, but whenever they asked her, she got all tongue-tied and ended up just shaking her head no.

Shelby was terrified at having to stand up in front of the class, or read out loud, or even raise her hand to go to the bathroom, anything that drew attention to herself. She wondered if it came from growing up as an only child, and living out on a farm where most of her companions were animals instead of humans. She wanted to hide in crowds, be someone that no one would notice. She never tried out for plays at school, or the band, or chorus or sports. Sooner or later, she'd make a mistake and everyone would look at her and start laughing. Just the thought of entering the contest, all those college people judging her work, made her hands sweat. And what if she won? There'd be more people looking at her picture, people interviewing her, and a television camera. Her mouth went dry. No, she could never do it.

"Maybe you're right," Mama said to Dad. "I think Shelby should enter that contest."

Later, while Dad read the newspaper and Mama wrote letters, Shelby went quietly to her room. She folded the contest announcement and stuffed it in a crack behind the chimney where her parents wouldn't find it. She hoped they wouldn't mention it again.

With her birthday just two days away, Shelby forgot about the contest and concentrated on her party. She wondered what her parents would give her. She'd been hinting for weeks that what she wanted most was an eighteen-speed, red mountain bike, one like her friend Jennifer had. The only bike Shelby'd had for years was the one-speed clunker her mother had had when she was a girl. Shelby was embarrassed to death to be seen riding it and whenever her friends asked her to go bike riding, she always said her bike was broken. Dad had said the new bike was too expensive and not to get her hopes up, but Shelby had seen a large cardboard box that looked bicycle-sized hidden under a tarp up in the rafters of the toolshed.

Shelby had planned her party, too. It wasn't going to be a big party, just her friends Julie, Katie and Jennifer, but Mama was going to take them all out for pizza, then to a movie and they'd come back home for dessert. She and Julie and Katie and Jennifer would stay up all night, talking and laughing, and in the morning she'd ride her new bike to the lake and they'd all spend the day at the beach. That's the way it was supposed to happen.

But on the night before her birthday, Mama got a call from Aunt Harriet. When Mama hung up the phone, there was a worried look on her face.

"Grandma's not feeling well and Harriet wondered if we could stay with her for a couple of days 'til she's feeling better."

Shelby couldn't believe what she was hearing. Mama must have forgotten about her birthday.

"Mama, my party's tomorrow!" she wailed.

"I know, Shelby, and I'm sorry. But Grandma needs us right now," Mama said.

"Why can't Aunt Harriet stay with her? She lives right near Grandma."

"Harriet would do it but she has a concert this weekend over in Burlington," Mama said. Aunt Harriet played piano for the Vermont Symphony Orchestra, and Shelby knew that was important to Aunt Harriet. But Shelby had other plans, too. Why were Aunt Harriet's plans more important than hers?

That evening, as they drove the twenty miles to Grandma's house, Shelby decided to punish Mama by not talking to her. But Mama didn't seem to notice. She chatted on and on about Mrs. Griffin's new baby and how Mr. Bemis had broken his hip and what color Eunice Atherton had painted her kitchen.

Like I care, Shelby thought.

"Now, Shelby," Mama said. "I don't want you sulking around Grandma and making her feel badly. She needs her rest. And good food. She probably got sick because she's not eating right. I don't think she's taking care of herself."

Shelby looked at Mama in surprise. Grandma

seemed perfectly capable of taking care of herself. And nobody was a better cook than Grandma.

"I hope I can talk Momma into coming to live with us," Mama went on. "She shouldn't be living alone anymore."

Shelby sat in stunned silence. Mama hadn't mentioned that before. There was no spare bedroom at their house, which could only mean one thing. She'd have to give up her room to Grandma and sleep on the couch.

They pulled into Grandma's yard with anger buzzing around Shelby's head like bees.

They found Grandma in bed. She looked pale, and she lifted an arm weakly.

"Harriet shouldn't have called you," she said. "It's nothing serious. I've just felt a little light-headed."

"I'm glad she called us," Mama said. Her tone was half-scolding. "You could have fallen."

She plumped Grandma's pillow.

"You know, Momma, I don't like the thought of you being here alone. It's time you came to live with us."

"Now, Carolyn, don't start up with that nonsense again," Grandma said. "I'm not that old, and I want to stay in my own house. All my happiest memories are here, with your father and you children."

Shelby breathed a sigh of relief. Her room was safe.

"I'm sorry it's so messy in here," Grandma said.

"Don't worry about anything, Momma," Mama said. "Shelby and I will be glad to straighten up the house."

Oh, great, thought Shelby. Instead of a party, I get to wash dishes and vacuum.

She sighed and Mama gave her a warning look.

"You seem upset, Shelby," Grandma said. "Is something bothering you?"

"I was supposed to have my birthday party tomorrow," Shelby said, not looking at her mother. "All my friends were going to come."

"Oh, dear," Grandma said. "I feel terrible that I ruined your plans."

"Now, Momma, we'll have Shelby's party when we get home," Mama said, glaring at Shelby. "We're happy to be here."

"Why don't we have a little celebration here?" Grandma said. "Just the three of us."

"No, thanks," Shelby said. "It wouldn't be the same."

She knew from the look on Mama's face she was in trouble and would be punished later, but she felt some satisfaction that Grandma felt badly, too.

Something brushed against her leg and she jumped back, startled.

A cat Shelby had never seen before, black with a white bib and paws, jumped on the bed, turned around once and curled up next to Grandma.

"When did you get a cat?" Shelby asked.

"He just showed up here a few weeks ago and settled right in like he'd always lived here," Grandma said. "He's good company." She scratched the cat under his chin and he began to purr.

"What's his name?" Shelby asked. She'd always wanted a cat but Dad was allergic to them.

"Rutherford," Grandma said.

For the first time since she'd gotten to Grandma's, Shelby laughed.

"What kind of name is that?" she asked. It sounded ridiculous to her.

"Rutherford B. Hayes was our nineteenth president," Grandma said.

"Was he president when you were a girl?" Shelby asked.

"Gracious, no!" Grandma said. "If that was the case, I'd be a hundred and thirteen now." She chuckled. "No, I just always thought it would be a good name for a cat. Very distinguished."

Shelby sat on the bed next to Grandma and stroked Rutherford's back. His fur was so soft. As she petted him, she was surprised to realize she didn't feel quite so angry.

"Would you like me to read to you?" she asked.

"That'd be lovely, dear," Grandma said, but before Shelby had opened the book on the bed table, Grandma's eyes had closed in sleep.

3

$\mathcal{G}$randma seemed a little better in the morning, and sat at the table for breakfast, but she tired quickly and Mama urged her to rest. Before she went back to bed, she pulled a package from her cupboard and handed it to Shelby.

"Here's a little something for your birthday," she said. "I'm sorry you missed your party."

The package had been wrapped with paper that had been folded many times. Grandma always saved gift paper and used it over and over again. Mama said it was because Grandma had grown up during the Depression.

Well, she won't be using this paper again, Shelby thought as she eagerly ripped the paper from the present.

It was a camera, but it wasn't a new camera. It was old, and boxy, and had scratches all over it and a dent in one corner. It looked so old Moses could have taken pictures with that camera. Shelby just stared at it, until Mama nudged her.

"Thanks, Grandma," Shelby said, sarcastically. Anger began to bubble up in her again, anger at Grandma for ruining her sleep-over and party, and anger at getting such a rotten gift. She still didn't know if she was getting her bike, but the way things were going, she doubted it. If they were giving her a great gift like a bike, Mama probably would have mentioned it.

She set the camera down hard on the table and ran out into the yard before she said something else Mama would punish her for.

Mama followed her outside.

"You know, Shelby, you could have been more gracious. You were rude to Grandma."

Shelby clenched her fists. Mama never understood how she felt.

"She gave me a crummy old camera, Mama," Shelby said. "It probably doesn't even work."

"It's not the gift, but the thought that counts," Mama said as all mothers do. Shelby thought there must be a Mother's Handbook somewhere that listed all the things mothers must say at least once before their children were grown, things like "Eat your vegetables," or "Don't run with scissors in your hand," or "If you can't say something nice, then don't say anything."

"That camera means a lot to Grandma," Mama said.

"It's a piece of junk," Shelby said, angrily. "Grandma was probably going to throw it away and decided to give it to me instead."

Mama sighed and shook her head.

"You know that's not true. But if you're going to be that way about it, you might as well stay outside. I don't want you coming in until you can be civil."

Shelby was determined that she'd *never* go in. She'd stay outside all day and night until Mama and Grandma got worried and begged her to come in.

Through the long afternoon, Shelby wandered the fields and woods around Grandma's. At first it was fun, exploring by herself. She found a whole series of dams that beavers had built down through the brook, she saw a fox and two kits playing at the edge of a field, and she ate some wild strawberries from the pasture, but by evening, she was sunburned and thirsty and ready for supper.

When Shelby went in, Grandma didn't say a word about the camera. Mama tried several times to start a conversation in her too-cheerful voice, then gave up and they ate supper together in uncomfortable silence.

Mama sent Grandma into the living room to rest and cleared off the table.

"I think I'll go out and get some air," she said. "Maybe this would be a good time for you to apologize."

When she left, Shelby sat sulking. She didn't think she had done anything to apologize for.

"Shelby, would you go into the hall closet and bring me the box that's underneath the stairs?" Grandma asked quietly.

Shelby hesitated. She didn't like going into the hall closet, especially at night. She used to be afraid of monsters lurking under the stairs. She didn't believe in monsters anymore, but the dark cubbyhole still made her nervous.

She opened the closet door, felt around under the stairs until she located the box, and carried it, half-running, to the living room.

"What's in here?" she asked.

"My photo albums," Grandma said.

Shelby sighed. Great. This evening would be even more boring than last night. Was she going to have to look at old photos of dead people she didn't even know?

But she didn't want to fight with Grandma anymore, she'd finished her book, and Grandma didn't have a television. Well, she had a television but you had to stand and hold the antenna to get any reception at all, and the picture was so fuzzy and grainy that it was hard to tell the actors from furniture.

Shelby sat beside Grandma on the couch as Grandma picked up the first album.

4

I grew up during the Depression," Grandma said, holding the album closed on her lap. "It was a time when people lost their jobs and a lot of folks went hungry. We had an orchard and garden, and Mama raised chickens so our family didn't go hungry, but there was no money for taxes. Papa didn't want to lose our farm, so he found work logging up in Canada. He was gone for months.

"While he was away, Mama said we should take pictures of all the things Papa would miss. Mama had an old Brownie camera and she bought film with her egg money. We took pictures of everything we could think of, from Rosie, our old cow, to the tree that blew down one night and flattened our farm wagon. It made the time go a little faster."

Shelby was quiet, thinking. She walked over to the table, picked up the camera and carried it back to where Grandma was sitting.

"Was this your Mama's camera?" she asked.

Grandma nodded.

"It was such a hard time for all of us, but fun, too, always thinking of new things we were going to show or tell Papa, and using the camera was exciting for us. I should have realized it was nothing a girl nowadays would want. I'm sorry."

"What happened when he came back?" Shelby asked.

Grandma's eyes sparkled, remembering.

"When Papa came home, you never saw such carrying on. We were all hugging him, and laughing and talking at once, and Mama was crying. Papa couldn't get over how we'd all grown. He spent hours looking at this photo album. We were so in the habit of taking pictures, we just kept on, even after Papa was home."

Grandma opened the album to a photograph of a man sitting on a chair in someone's yard. He was holding a pig on his lap. It was the biggest pig Shelby had ever seen.

"Wow!" Shelby said. "Who is that?"

"That's my brother Ernest, holding our pig, Elmer," Grandma said.

"Why was he holding it on his lap?" Shelby asked.

"I have no idea," Grandma said. "It probably had something to do with showing off to his friends."

Grandma turned another page.

"Here's one of Papa standing next to the 1940 Ford. Two years earlier, the 1938 hurricane had come through and blown down most of the maple trees we'd sugared from. It made you want to cry, seeing all those beautiful old trees laid down like matchsticks. That syrup money had been paying taxes and buying us new school shoes every year. But as Papa said, 'No use crying over spilt milk or uprooted trees,' so he went to cutting up all those trees, and made enough money on the lumber to pay taxes and buy that

car. Only new car he ever had. Doesn't he look proud!"

And he did, leaning against the car, with his hat at an angle and a big grin on his face. Shelby could see where her Uncle Earl took after his grandfather.

She pointed to the next photograph of a girl standing on the backs of two horses, one foot on each horse. Underneath, someone had written "CIRCUS GIRL!"

"Who's that?" Shelby asked.

Grandma laughed.

"Me," she said.

"That's you?" Shelby said. She couldn't imagine Grandma as a young girl doing something so daring.

"Don't look so surprised," Grandma said. "I wasn't always this old, you know."

Shelby flipped through more pages.

"Don't you have any color pictures?" she asked.

"I have photos of you and Harriet's boys that are all in color," Grandma said. "But when I was a girl, there wasn't any color film. All photographs were black and white. But when I look at these pictures, I remember the colors. Papa had hair the color of wheat, and eyes as brown as butternuts. That coat I'm wearing as the circus girl was bought new for my sister Virginia but it was too small so they saved it for me. Since I always got hand-me-downs, I loved having something that hadn't been worn before. And it was bright red, my favorite color."

Shelby and Grandma were so involved in the album they didn't hear the soft thud of the screen door and they both jumped when Mama spoke.

"What are you two doing?" she asked.

"We're looking at Grandma's old photos," Shelby said eagerly, flipping through the pages. "Come look at them, Mama. This is her brother Ernest and his pig, Elmer. Did you ever see such a humongous pig? That picture is of her father and his new car and do you know who that is standing on those horses? It's Grandma! Can you believe it?"

Grandma and Mama looked at each other and smiled as the words tumbled out of Shelby's mouth. She came to the last pages of the album and stopped, confused. One of the photographs showed a tall, lean man standing beside a white horse.

"Except I don't know who this is," Shelby said.

"That's your Grandpa," Grandma said softly. There was pride in her voice. "I met Arthur at a dance when I was seventeen. All the girls were smitten with him and they were all flirting with him, hoping he'd ask them to dance. I knew I didn't stand a chance so I sat over by the coats reading *Wuthering Heights*. I heard my name and I looked up to see him standing in front of me. He held out his hand and I took it," Grandma said, her eyes far away. "We were married for forty-two years, but every time I looked at him, I saw that dashing boy of nineteen who walked across that floor and asked me to dance."

Grandma shook her head a little, bringing herself back to the present.

"I talk too much," she said. "I'm sure I'm boring you with all my stories."

"No, you're not," Shelby said quickly. "You know, it's kind of funny, I mean, I never cared much for old photographs. Just seemed like a bunch of old dead people. But hearing you talk about them makes them seem real."

Grandma smiled.

"I'm glad," she said. "Because they were real. They were wonderful people and I want you to know about them."

"I like hearing the stories about them again, too," Mama said. "For years, I've been meaning to get copies made of those old photos and have you write on them who the people are and what years the pictures were taken."

"We'll have to do that, one of these days," Grandma said.

The mantel clock chimed ten o'clock.

"It's way past bedtime, Shelby," Mama said gently.

"For both of us," Grandma said, closing the album. "We can look at more of these tomorrow."

Shelby picked up the camera again and began to climb the stairs to her room, then ran back to give Grandma a hug.

"Thanks, Grandma," she said. "I'm glad you gave me the camera."

5

$\mathcal{A}$fter he finished morning milking, Dad drove up to spend the day with them. Shelby ran to greet him; it seemed like weeks since she'd been home.

Dad grinned as he pulled a box from the back seat and held it out to her.

"Happy Birthday," he said. "A day late."

As she took in the size of the box, Shelby's heart sank into her socks. Her gift was definitely not a bike.

The box contained a stereo cassette player, a gift she'd asked for five years ago.

"I hope it's the kind you wanted," Dad said, and Shelby didn't have the heart to tell him that cassettes were practically obsolete now. Why couldn't parents keep track of things like that? Most of her friends had CD players now. Still, it would be good to play music she liked in her room instead of having to listen to that mushy junk her mom and dad played.

"Thanks, Dad," she said, hugging him, and walked him into the house.

As they all sat down to breakfast together, Grandma announced she was going to church.

"Church?" Mama said. "Don't you think you should stay home and rest?"

"Can't," Grandma said. "I'm doing a solo in the choir today."

"A solo?" Mama sounded like Grandma's echo. "But, Momma, you've been sick. They can get someone else to do the solo."

"Now, Carolyn, quit fussing," Grandma said. "I'll be fine. It'll do me good to see everyone at church."

They finished eating, and Mama and Shelby went to change into their church clothes. Dad settled into Grandma's wing chair. He pulled out his pipe, put his feet up on the coffee table, and picked up the Sunday paper that he'd brought with him.

Grandma fixed a hawklike stare on him.

"I was expecting we'd all go together," she said.

Dad didn't care for church anymore than he did for vegetables. He stared at her, then grinned.

"Okay, I surrender," he said, setting down his pipe and paper. "Bring your camera along," he called to Shelby. "After church we'll run by the store to see if they still carry that kind of film."

Grandma went to the Presbyterian church in East Craftsbury. It was a beautiful brown-shingled church with large stained-glass windows and a row of old maple trees that lined the driveway. It was the only brown church Shelby had ever seen. She liked how the church was surrounded by green fields, and she wondered if the cows grazing in those fields ever paused on Sunday mornings to listen to the music.

As they drove up, Grandma pointed to the white house off to the left of the church.

"That's the manse," she said, "where the minister lives. Back in the fifties, Alfred Hitchcock filmed part of his movie *The Trouble with Harry* there."

While Shelby was wondering who Alfred Hitchcock was, Mama joined in.

"The colors were beautiful that fall," she said. She turned toward Shelby.

"Did you know I was an extra in the movie?" she asked.

"You were in a movie, Mama?"

"Oh, I'm only visible for a second," Mama said, "and I was only five years old, but it was pretty exciting. Of course, nothing like that had ever happened up here before."

In the yard, a group of women clustered around Grandma, asking about her health and telling her how glad they were to see her. They seemed to give Grandma strength. She stood straighter and had more color in her cheeks. And they made her laugh. Shelby could see why Grandma liked being with them.

A woman who'd just arrived slipped into the group.

"Edna, how are you feeling?" she asked. "We heard you were sick this week."

"Fine, fine," Grandma said briskly, waving off her illness as if it were a swarm of flies. "Agnes, you remember Carolyn, my daughter, her husband, Frank, and my granddaughter, Shelby?"

"Of course," said Agnes. "How wonderful to see all of you. I'm glad you could join us today. You're in for a real treat, hearing Edna sing. But I suspect you hear her sing all the time."

No, we don't, Shelby thought. This day was full of surprises, finding out Mama had been in a movie and that Grandma sang solos. She couldn't remember *ever* hearing Grandma sing. Was she the only one who didn't know about it? She looked at Mama and was somewhat relieved to see that Mama looked as bewildered as she felt.

The bell in the steeple rang, and everyone filed into church.

Inside was cool, and the pattern of light through the stained-glass windows played over the wooden pews and floor. Shelby, Grandma, Dad, and Mama slid into a pew just as the organ began to play.

The children's choir sang "This Little Light of Mine" and then the minister asked them to bow their heads in prayer. With her head bowed, Shelby glanced up at Grandma.

Grandma looked nervous. Shelby looked at the bulletin in her hand and saw that Grandma's solo came next. She tried to imagine what it would be like to stand up in front of this crowd of people and sing. Just the thought of it made her dizzy. How could Grandma do it?

The prayer ended and all eyes turned toward Grandma. Grandma stood up quickly and stepped to the front of the choir. She nodded to the organist and looked back out over the sea of faces. Well, not exactly a sea, Shelby thought, more like a pond.

Grandma gave a little smile to Shelby, took a deep breath and began to sing.

The hymn was "Amazing Grace." Grandma sang the first verse alone, not even the organ joining in, just Grandma's voice rising into the peak of the ceiling, filling the church with its clear sweetness.

No one made a sound; even the babies hushed. The words, and the way Grandma sang, sent a delicious shiver through Shelby and she felt the hair stand up on her arms.

Amazing Grace, how sweet the sound
That saved a wretch like me.
I once was lost but now am found
Was blind, but now I see.

On the second verse, the organ accompanied her, on the third verse, the rest of the choir joined in, but on the last verse, Grandma sang alone again.

When we've been there 10,000 years
Bright shining as the sun,
We've no less time to sing God's praise
Than when we first begun.

When she finished, and the last few notes seemed to linger in the air, there was appreciative silence. No one wanted to disturb the sense of peace that Grandma had created.

Reluctantly, it seemed, the minister began his sermon. He read from Matthew 5, something about a light hidden under a bushel, and salt, and then spoke about how everyone had special gifts. He spoke for a long time. Shelby got restless and ended up counting all the panes in the stained-glass windows. The backs of her legs

were sweaty from sitting so long, and twice she saw Mama poke Dad in the ribs to wake him up. She did hear the minister finish by saying, "Now go out, and let your light shine throughout the world," and wondered what he meant by that, but she didn't wonder long she was so glad the service was over and people began to file out of the church into the bright sunlight.

6

$\mathcal{E}$veryone crowded around Grandma, congratulating her. Shelby slipped in beside Grandma and waited for a break in the conversation.

"Weren't you scared, Grandma?" she asked.

"Terrified," Grandma said, squeezing her hand. "But it's the waiting at the beginning that's the worst. Once I start singing, the good Lord takes over and I'm all right."

At the back of the church, Grandma introduced them all to Reverend McDaniels. He shook Shelby's hand.

"Your grandmother has a beautiful voice," he said. "We deeply appreciate the gift of music she shares with us."

"Just trying to let my light shine," Grandma said, smiling, and Shelby got a hint of what the minister had meant.

Uncle Earl threw an arm around Grandma's shoulders.

"That was beautiful, Momma," he said. "I wish I'd inherited your ability to sing. I can't carry a tune in a bucket."

"You have a fine voice, Earl, and you know it," Grandma said, half-scolding. "But you have other talents."

Uncle Earl turned toward Shelby.

"Speaking of talent, have you drawn anything for the contest yet?"

"What contest?" Grandma asked, looking at Shelby. Shelby squirmed.

"The creamery's having an art contest to celebrate its 75th anniversary," Uncle Earl said. "I thought Shelby might want to enter."

"It's the first I've heard of it," Grandma said. "Sounds like a wonderful idea."

"You might want to come 'round the creamery soon," Uncle Earl said, still talking to Shelby. "We've started adding some flavors to our butter. Thought you might like to see how we do it." Shelby nodded and Uncle Earl grinned.

"I'll take you next week, then," he said, and left for home.

Most of the other people had left, too, but Shelby could see Mama and Dad under the maple trees, talking with people they hadn't seen in years.

"I'm not entering that contest, Grandma," Shelby said, quietly.

"Whyever not?" Grandma said. "It'd be a good opportunity for you."

"I just don't want to," Shelby said. Grandma wouldn't understand.

"Is that the real reason?" Grandma asked.

Shelby's feelings of pride in Grandma were quickly replaced by irritation. Why couldn't Grandma just drop the subject and leave her alone?

"I think you're afraid," Grandma said. "You shouldn't be."

Shelby bit her lip. She wanted to tell Grandma to mind her own business. Grandma had no right telling Shelby how she should or shouldn't be. She'd already ruined Shelby's birthday. She didn't have to ruin this day, too.

"You're so shy," Grandma said. "You need to try to get over that, and I think entering that contest would help build up your confidence. Besides, there's not a thing in the world to be afraid of."

Her words pushed Shelby's anger to the surface.

"That's easy for you to say," Shelby shouted. The words tumbled out before she could rein them in, and the last few people in the church yard turned to look. Even Mama looked in their direction, her face showing concern. In a moment, she'd be over, wondering why Shelby was shouting at her grandmother and she'd have to stick her two cents in, too. Shelby's face reddened and she lowered her voice.

"You're so strong and brave. You've always known what you wanted to do and you just went and did it. I'm not like that."

Grandma was silent for a few moments, thinking.

"That's not true," she said, quietly. "So much

of my life I haven't been brave at all. I was afraid to make decisions, or I let other people make my decisions for me, and when I did make a decision, I was afraid to follow it through. I just don't want you to make the same mistakes I made. You're a gifted person; I want you to let your light shine. I want you to follow your dreams, to take risks, to not be afraid."

Shelby couldn't imagine Grandma ever being afraid.

"Don't get me wrong," Grandma continued. "I've had a good life and a wonderful family, but there are things I wish I could change."

"Like what?" Shelby asked. She wanted to know, but she wasn't sure Grandma would tell her.

"I always wanted to go to college," Grandma said. "In high school, I was at the top of my class, and I wanted to be the first girl in our family to go to college. But then my mother died and I had to help support the family. I got a job as a telephone operator and worked there until I met your grandfather. We got married, the children were born and my dreams of college got replaced with the responsibilities of being a wife and mother. When the time came that I could have gone, after Arthur died and the children were grown, I was too scared to go."

"Why don't you go now?" Shelby asked.

"Now?" Grandma hooted. "At my age? Wouldn't the teachers and other students get a laugh at that!"

Shelby couldn't believe what she'd heard. Grandma had just sung in front of a whole church full of people but she was still afraid of being laughed at. Maybe she and Grandma weren't so different after all.

"I guess we're finally ready to go," Mama announced.

"We?" said Dad. "I was ready forty minutes ago."

Mama gave him a playful poke in the side.

"I noticed you were doing your share of visiting, too," she said.

They swung by the store. No they didn't carry that particular kind of film anymore, but the owner was sure it was still available. "We'll get some next time we're in Burlington," Dad said.

On the way back to Grandma's house, Mama began humming "Amazing Grace." When she realized what she was doing, she turned her head and stared accusingly at Grandma.

"You know, Momma, I'm quite cross with you, keeping your singing a secret. Why didn't you tell me?"

"Afraid, I guess," Grandma said.

"You never sang in the choir when we were growing up," Mama said.

"I had too many of you children to tend to, for one thing," Grandma said. "And for another, I was too shy." She squeezed Shelby's hand. "But I guess I'm getting braver in my old age."

"I'm feeling much better today," Grandma continued. "When we get home, I think I'll go out to the garden and pick some peas for dinner. Not having picked them all week, I've probably got oodles of them. Won't they taste wonderful with some fresh raspberries for dessert?"

Grandma, Mama, and Dad began discussing the gardens they passed, who had the tallest peas and whose corn was tasselling. While they talked, Shelby aimed the camera out the window and pretended she was a world-famous photo-journalist. As soon as she got some film, she'd start putting together her own photo album.

Peering through the view finder, the woods, barns, and fields whizzing by so fast it made her dizzy, she noticed smoke rising above a line of trees. She lowered the camera.

"What's that?" she asked, and Dad, Mama, and Grandma turned their heads to look.

Dad looked at Mama and drove faster. Grandma leaned forward and gripped the back of the front seat so tightly her knuckles turned white.

They came over the crest of Breezy Hill, and they could see it, smoke billowing fifty feet into the air and flames writhing like snakes.

Grandma's house was burning.

7

$\mathcal{D}$ad drove to a neighbor's house and called the fire department, but it was too late. By the time the fire engines arrived, the house had begun to collapse.

Grandma, Dad, Mama, and Shelby stood a safe distance away, but even so, Shelby could feel the heat sear her face. They watched the roof cave in, sending up a shudder of sparks, and the flames climbed and blackened the walls.

Grandma put an arm around Shelby's shoulders.

"Don't cry, child," Grandma said. "It's only

wood. I'm just thankful no one was hurt."

But Shelby couldn't help but think of all of Grandma's things that had burned, things that Grandma cared for: the mantel clock that her great-grandfather had made, the chair her grandmother had brought from Scotland, and all those old photographs of the people Grandma loved. They could never be replaced.

Shelby went through each room in her mind, remembering it. The simple things that had given each room beauty: the blue Mason jars that Grandma kept filled with wildflowers; the old upright piano where Aunt Harriet had practiced for years; the four-poster bed in Grandma's bedroom, covered by the nine-patch quilt that had taken Grandma months to piece when she was thirteen. And on that quilt a beautiful black cat with a white bib.

Shelby gasped and searched Grandma's face.

"What about Rutherford?" she asked. "Was he in the house?"

Grandma caught her breath, then nodded.

"Maybe he got out somehow," Dad said, but even he sounded doubtful.

Shelby squeezed Grandma's hand and hot

tears stung her throat as she watched the fire eat the last of the house. She thought how awful it would be to be trapped in there, the smoke and flames getting nearer and nearer, and not being able to get out. She pictured Rutherford running from room to room, scratching at the front door and finally hiding under Grandma's bed until. . . .

She shuddered. She didn't want to think about it. Poor Rutherford.

Since the house was a total loss, the firemen had turned their attention to saving the barn. They sprayed water over the roof and the walls facing the house until they were sure stray sparks weren't going to ignite the barn.

One of the volunteer firemen came over to where they were standing, his face black with soot.

"Any idea how it might have started?" he asked.

Grandma shook her head, then raised a hand to her mouth as a thought came to her.

"You don't think I left the stove on, do you?" Grandma asked.

"I don't think so. I was in the kitchen, too,

and would have noticed," Mama said. "But that's one reason we don't want you living alone. We want to be there to help watch out for you."

Shelby thought that was a low blow. Grandma wasn't forgetful and Mama was using this crisis to try to get Grandma to live with them. Besides, how well had they watched out for Grandma? The house had burned down even with them there visiting her. No, she didn't think Grandma was responsible for the fire, but she was afraid Dad might be. Shelby remembered the pipe that Dad had left by Grandma's chair to go to church.

Another fireman walked over.

"I was just nosing around, seeing if I could come up with what caused it," he said. "Probably have to let things cool down some before we can really get in there to check it out."

"Mike, could it have been started by my pipe?" Dad asked, and Shelby realized that Dad remembered setting the pipe down, too. She also realized it must have been pretty hard for Dad to ask that question, to admit he might be the one who'd destroyed Grandma's house.

"Your pipe?" Mike asked.

"I left it on the table in the living room," Dad said.

Mike shook his head.

"I don't think so," he said. "It looks like the fire started in the cellar. My guess is it was caused by old wiring."

Dad breathed a sigh of relief.

"Edna, I'm sorry your house burned, but I'm glad to know I didn't cause it. I'd have a hard time living with myself. I guess if anything good came out of this it's that I'm giving up smoking for good."

The firemen began folding up their hoses and loading their equipment back onto the trucks.

"What will Grandma do now?" Shelby whispered to her mother, but Grandma overheard.

"Harriet will be coming home from Burlington tonight," she answered. "I'll stay with her."

Before she knew what she was doing, Shelby squeezed Grandma's hand and said, "No, Grandma, I want you to stay with us," and was surprised to feel she meant it.

"Let's go home, Momma," Mama said, gently, drawing Grandma toward the car. Grandma seemed too tired to argue. As they got into the car, Mama slipped Shelby a grateful smile.

They rode home in silence. Grandma looked old and defeated. Shelby couldn't think of a thing to say to her. Nothing she said would change what had happened.

Home had a new meaning for her. She decided it was one of the most wonderful words ever created, a word that carried with it a sense of warmth and safety, a sense of belonging. Where did Grandma belong now? she wondered.

Shelby ran into her home before the others. She went from room to room, touching items that suddenly seemed more precious to her, grateful that home was as she'd left it.

"Momma, you'll be in Shelby's room," Mama said. "Shelby can sleep on the couch."

"Oh, no," Grandma said. "I'm not going to kick Shelby out of her own room."

"It's okay, Grandma," Shelby said, "I don't mind, really I don't. I'm glad you're here."

Mama suddenly remembered they hadn't eaten since breakfast. She sliced some bread and fresh cucumbers, but Grandma wasn't hungry.

"You should eat, Momma," Mama said.

Shelby thought Mama should let Grandma be.

"She's too sad to eat, Mama," Shelby said. "She misses her home."

Grandma touched Shelby's cheek and tried to smile, but her eyes were dark and they didn't sparkle the way they usually did when she smiled.

"What I'll miss most is that silly cat and my photo albums," Grandma said.

"I'm sorry they're gone," Shelby said. "I don't like seeing you so sad."

Grandma patted Shelby's shoulder.

"Don't be worrying about me," she said. "I'll be right as rain in a couple of days. I'll bounce back."

But she didn't bounce back. She hardly spoke over the next few days and just picked at her food.

One night, when Shelby got up to go to the bathroom, she noticed the door to her room was open. She tiptoed to the threshold and peeked in.

Grandma sat at the window, staring out.

Moonlight spilled into the room, painting Grandma with silvery light.

"Are you all right, Grandma?" Shelby asked.

Grandma jumped a little, but didn't turn around.

"I miss Arthur especially on nights like this," Grandma said. "Sometimes, your grandfather and I had picnics at night. I know that sounds funny, having a picnic at night, but with eight children, it was the only chance we got to be alone together, when they were all asleep. I'd fix us a basket of cold chicken, biscuits, and pickles—your grandfather always loved pickles—and we'd sit up on the hill behind the barn and talk about whatever was on our minds.

"Some nights we had a big old full moon shining down on us and we didn't even need to light a lantern. I even remember a few winter nights when there was enough light from the stars to see by. We didn't need the moon."

Grandma absentmindedly twisted her wedding ring around her finger as she spoke.

"Remembering those nights has made me think of something I heard your grandfather once quote, from William Cowper, I think,

'What peaceful hours I once enjoy'd!
   How sweet their mem'ry still!
But they have left an aching void,
   The world can never fill.' "

Grandma sat quietly for a moment before she continued.

"Losing your grandfather was the hardest thing I ever had to endure. But losing the house where your grandfather and I lived and raised our family has made me feel like I've lost a part of him all over again."

Shelby wished she could say something comforting but she had no idea what that would be.

"You know what I said last Sunday about letting your light shine?" Grandma said. "Well, it feels like my light has just about gone out."

Shelby's heart ached. She felt helpless.

"I love you, Grandma," was all she could think to say, but it brought Grandma back to the present.

"I love you, too, Shelby," she said gently. "And thank you; you're a good listener. Go back to bed now. I'll be all right."

Shelby went back to bed, but lay awake,

thinking of ways she could help. Maybe if she could get Grandma to talk some more, Grandma would feel better.

She tried the next evening.

$\mathcal{W}$ould you tell me some stories about Grandpa and Ernest?" she asked.

"I'm too tired tonight, honey," Grandma said. "Could we do it another night?"

But Grandma was too tired the next night and the night after that.

"Give her some time," Mama said. "She'll work through it in her own time."

But Shelby wanted to do more than just sit and wait for Grandma to get better on her own. Was there anything she could do to cheer up Grandma? Grandma had said she missed Rutherford and her albums most. Well, Shelby couldn't bring Rutherford back, or the photographs either, but maybe she could do the next best thing.

8

When she wasn't feeding calves, and picking peas in the garden, Shelby spent much of the next week in the attic. It must have been a hundred degrees up there, but it was the only place she felt she could work without being disturbed.

At first, Mama didn't say anything, but as the week wore on, she began to worry.

"It's such a nice day, Shelby, don't you want to go for a bike ride?" she'd ask.

"Maybe tomorrow, Mama."

Or, "Your dad and I thought we'd drive over to an auction in Irasburg. Wouldn't you like to come along?"

"Not today, Mama. I'm busy."

"Busy with what? Why are you spending so much time up in the attic?"

"I'm working on something."

"Can't you tell me what it is?" Mama asked.

Shelby shook her head. Mama studied her.

"Shelby, are you all right?"

"Yes, Mama. I'm just working on something."

On Saturday afternoon, she came down from the attic carrying a photo album. She laid the album in Grandma's lap.

"What's this?" Grandma asked.

"Pictures I drew all week." Shelby said.

"You've been drawing all this time?" Mama said. Shelby nodded.

"Why?" Grandma asked.

"You'll see," Shelby said. "I made them for you."

Grandma opened the album.

The first picture showed a man holding a pig on his lap.

"Why, that's Ernest and Elmer!" Grandma exclaimed. Her hand trembled as she turned the page. "And here's Papa and his new car!"

"I know," Shelby said. "I drew them just as I remembered them from your old photos."

Grandma began to cry. Shelby didn't know what to say. She'd meant to make Grandma feel better, not cry. But then Grandma began to laugh.

"Oh, Shelby, you have a gift, a real gift," she said. "You've caught Ernest's expression just perfect. Ernest always said he never expected that pig to be so heavy."

They all heard the sound of a car in the driveway.

"Why, that's Frank," Mama said. "I wondered where he'd gone off to." She stepped out onto the porch to meet him.

Shelby turned back to Grandma and the album.

"Look at the last picture," she said.

Grandma looked at it and caught her breath. Shelby had drawn Grandma in a graduation cap and gown. In her right hand she held a diploma.

"Oh, Shelby," Grandma said.

"All the other pictures are of your past," Shelby said, shyly. "I thought there should be one of your future. You're not too old. Julie said her great-aunt got her college degree when she was eighty-two!"

Only Dad and Mama's entrance prevented Grandma from crying again. She wiped her eyes as they strode into the room. Mama was still trying to figure out where Dad had been.

Dad sneezed.

"I've been up to your mother's," he said. He sneezed again.

Mama eyed him suspiciously.

"What's gotten into you?" she asked. "That sounds like your allergy kicking up. You haven't been around any cats, have you?"

"Well, as a matter of fact, I have," Dad said, gleefully, and pulled out something from underneath his jacket, something that was black and white and kicking and yowling. Shelby couldn't have been more surprised if he'd pulled a rabbit from a hat.

"Rutherford!" she cried.

Rutherford leaped out of Dad's arms and into

Grandma's lap, right on top of the album. He rubbed his nose against Grandma's cheek and yowled again as if trying to tell her what had happened to him.

"Land sakes!" Grandma exclaimed, petting him until he purred. "I can't believe he's alive. Wherever did you find him?"

Dad was grinning like the Cheshire cat himself, even though his eyes were red and watery.

"I was getting ready to come home when I heard a meow and out of the barn walked Rutherford. He must have escaped the house, somehow, during the fire, and hidden out in the barn."

They all stared at Rutherford in wonder. Shelby wished he could talk so he could tell them how he'd escaped.

"I had another surprise out at your place, Edna," Dad said, looking at Mama. "A bunch of your friends were there."

"Whatever for?" Grandma asked.

"It seems the people in your church are building you a house," Dad said.

Grandma sat up quickly, almost upsetting

Rutherford who clutched at her blouse with his claws.

"They had the frame walls up," Dad said, "and I helped them put up the rafters while I was there and they're going to start Monday with putting on the roof."

Grandma sank back into her chair.

"Oh, my," she said, shaking her head slowly. "Those good people. How will I ever be able to repay them?"

"You already have," Dad said. "They all said you and Arthur had done so much for them all these years, this was something they could do in return."

Grandma kept shaking her head and Shelby was pondering on the wonderous events of Rutherford's return and Grandma's house being rebuilt when Mama broke the spell.

"Well, that's ridiculous," Mama said. She glared at Dad. "You'll just have to drive up there on Monday to tell them to stop building and that Momma's going to stay right here with us."

"You're not going to tell them any such thing," Grandma said, sternly. "I'll be moving back to my house as soon as it's built."

Mama started to protest, but Grandma held up her hand.

"Now, Carolyn, I'm not going to argue with you. I'm grateful to you for wanting me to stay with you, but I want to live by myself, in my own home, for as long as I'm able. When you get to be my age, you'll understand. Independence is important."

Mama wasn't one to give up easily.

"Momma, what will you do out there all by yourself?"

Grandma smiled, and it seemed to Shelby there was a twinkle in her eye.

"Oh, I'm going to be very busy. You see, I've decided something else, too. I'm going to college."

Mama looked like she'd been hit with a rock.

"College? At your age? You can't be serious."

"I'm very serious," Grandma said. "It's something I always wanted, but I didn't think I could do it. Now I think I can."

"I can't believe you're thinking of doing this," Mama said. "Who put this idea into your head?"

Grandma reached out and took Shelby's hand.

"My partner in crime," she said, laughing, and in that laugh, Shelby saw a glimmer of light returning.

The idea came to Shelby that night as she lay in her room. (Grandma had insisted that since she wouldn't be staying much longer, Shelby should have her room back.) Shelby crept out of bed and sat at her desk. She took a deep breath and began to draw.

The picture had been in her mind all evening, exactly as she'd seen in Grandma's photos, the one of Grandpa loading milk cans onto the back of his 1942 truck to take them to the creamery. The photograph had burned along with all the others, but Shelby remembered it clearly. She didn't know why she hadn't thought of it sooner. It would celebrate the creamery's history. If she worked on it most of the night, she could have it done by tomorrow, just in time for the contest deadline.

Probably, almost definitely, she would not win. But now, like Grandma, she had the courage to try.

For the first time, she saw that she could choose who and how she wanted to be. She didn't have to be old scared Shelby anymore. This year, in a new grade, she'd try out her new self. She was going to go out for the soccer team, maybe join the Photography Club, be braver, so that later, when she was Grandma's age, she could look back and say, "Yes, I've led an interesting life, and I wouldn't change a minute of it."

In the morning, she'd ask Grandma if she wanted to go on a picnic, just the two of them, tomorrow night. They'd pack a supper and sit upon the hill under the stars to tell stories, plan their futures, and talk about whatever else was on their minds.